Pet Riddles and Jokes

with Franny and Frank

written by
Lisa Eisenberg

illustrated by
Scott Scheidly

HARCOURT BRACE & COMPANY

Orlando Atlanta Austin Boston San Francisco Chicago Dallas New York
Toronto London

His front teeth!

What kind of fish are in the sky?

Starfish!

My cat ate some yarn.

How is she?

Fine. But she just had mittens!

Oops! I think I just stepped on my cat's foot.
What did she say?